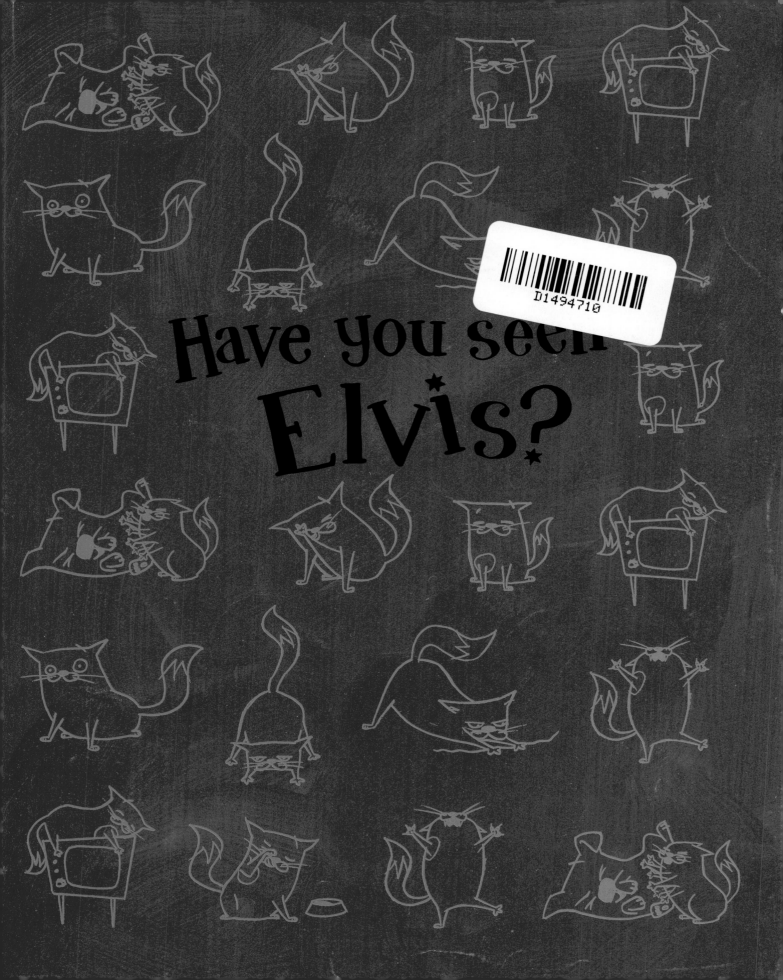

Have you seen Elvis?

For Trevor and Minty – N.S.

First published 2003 by Macmillan Children's Books
This edition published 2013 by Macmillan Children's Books
A division of Macmillan Publishers Limited
20 New Wharf Road, London N1 9RR
Basingstoke and Oxford

Associated companies throughout the world

www.panmacmillan.com

ISBN: 978-0-333-98708-7

Text copyright © Andrew Murray 2003
Illustrations copyright © Nicola Slater 2003

7 9 8
A CIP catalogue record for this book is available from the British Library.

Printed in China

ANDREW MURRAY

Have you seen Elvis?

Illustrated by NICOLA SLATER

MACMILLAN CHILDREN'S BOOKS

Buddy the dog and Elvis the cat were

ALWAYS FIGHTING.

Whenever Buddy was eating, Elvis would pounce, with a

RRRAAAOUMMMMM

and a scratch of his claws.

Whenever Elvis was sleeping, Buddy would pounce with a

WOAH WOAH WOAH

and a snap of his jaws.

and they
FOUGHT
and FOUGHT
and FOUGHT.

"This fighting is wearing me out," grumbled Elvis.
"I'VE HAD ENOUGH."

And that evening he crept out through the
cat-flap . . . and didn't come back.

When Elvis still wasn't back the next morning,
Lucy searched all through the house and all around the garden.

the
washing machine

the
dustbin

the
laundry
basket

the bushes

the
hat stand

She Looked
everywhere!

"Perhaps he'll turn up when he's hungry," she thought.

So she put out a big saucer of Elvis's favourite food – kippers. But still Elvis didn't come back.

Lucy made posters
and put them up
all over town.

She asked the neighbours
if they'd seen Elvis,
but no one had.

Poor Lucy was very upset. Her eyes were all red and puffy from crying. Buddy felt guilty.

It's ALL my fault. If I hadn't fought with Elvis, he wouldn't have run away.

Buddy tried to comfort Lucy. He put his paw on her lap and licked her hand. But she shooed him away.

sleep on top of the television...

I can't believe it. I think I miss him.

That night, when Lucy had gone to bed, BUDDY squeezed through the cat-flap and set out into the darkness.

Buddy soon realised he wasn't alone.
Alley cats were all around him,
hissing and spitting and caterwauling.

"Stupid dog," they hissed.
"You don't belong here. This is
the night, and it belongs to us."
Closer they came, closer
                  and closer . . .

"Wait!" said Buddy.
"I don't want any trouble.
I'm just looking for a . . . a *friend*.
He's called Elvis."

The alley cats stopped. "Elvis?" they said,
in surprise. "You're a friend of Elvis's?"
"Yes," said Buddy. "He's
gone missing, and we're
worried about him . . ."

"WELL, WHY DIDN'T YOU SAY SO?"

the cats laughed.

"Elvis is a friend of ours, too.
Come on, we'll help you find him."

Buddy and the alley
cats searched
through the night.
Buddy tried his best to
keep up as they looked
under bushes and cars,
on roofs, in trees and
in all the gardens and
streets and alleys.

By dawn they were
exhausted.
"Oh, dear," sighed Buddy.
"Where can Elvis be?"
Just then,
there was
a gust
of wind.

Buddy lifted his nose.
He sniffed.
He could smell something.
Something that reminded him of . . .

ELVIS!

Oh, wow!

"LEAVE ME ALONE,"

said Elvis.

"I don't want to fight
any more."

"I haven't come to FIGHT you, Elvis," said Buddy.
"It's just . . . Lucy's worried about you and, well . . .
I was worried, too.

"Please come
home."

Elvis looked at him
suspiciously.

"Don't worry, Elvis," called the alley cats.

"YOU CAN TRUST HIM!"

"ELVIS, YOU'RE BACK!" shouted Lucy.

She stroked and stroked him. And she gave Buddy a big hug.
"Now . . . " she said, "I'm going to get us all some breakfast.
Can I leave you two alone for one minute, without you fighting?"

Lucy came out of the kitchen with lots
of toast, kippers and doggie chews.

"Breakfast!" she called.
But there was no reply.

She peeped round the door
and smiled.

"I don't think I need
to worry any more."